A Night of Dark Intent

by L. Don Swartz

Baker's Plays
7611 Sunset Blvd.
Los Angeles, CA 90042
bakersplays.com

A NIGHT OF DARK INTENT was originally produced by Starry Night Theatre, Inc., at the Ghostlight Theatre in North Tonawanda, New York on October 2, 2008. The production, directed by L. Don Swartz, featured the following cast:

MIRANDA . . . . Colleen Neuman

WILMA. . . . . Joy Ann Wrona

INGRID . . . . Julie Senko

HOLLY . . . . .Vanessa Stipkovits

MRS. THURMIN . . . . Sharon Priest

GRETCHEN. . . . . .Justine Swartz

DEPUTY TERRY . . . . Mollie McDermott

LENORA STARK . . . . Joann V. Mis

SHERIFF WATKINS . . . . .Jesse Swartz

RADIO BROADCASTER . . . . .James Laski

CHARACTERS

MIRANDA – (mature) A psychic with genuine gifts. She keeps having visions of her own bloody future in the house of Stark.

WILMA – (30s-40s) A theatre technician and outspoken feminist with self-proclaimed homicidal inclinations.

INGRID – (30s-40s) An actress playing a serial killer who has gotten too close to her character.

HOLLY – (20-ish) A playwright who has come to the house of Stark to reconcile a sometimes nightmarish childhood.

MRS. THURMIN – (mature) A church secretary who knows more than she is telling about the night the Starks were butchered.

GRETCHEN – (20-ish) A hitchhiker who mysteriously appears on the side of the road near the Stark house.

DEPUTY TERRY – (20-ish) One of Chestnut Hollow's finest, who finds herself out of her league when she comes face-to-face with a serial killer.

LENORA STARK – (30s-40s) A convicted serial killer who escapes from the State asylum for the criminally Insane.

SHERIFF WATKINS (recorded voice)

RADIO BROADCASTER (recorded voice)

These are REAL people. Not types. The acting style is realistic.

SETTING

The abandoned Stark family home, on the outskirts of Chestnut Hollow, New York

TIME

October, 1978

For Agatha Christie

She knows why.

ACT I

Scene One

(*SETTING: The Stark family home. An empty house on the outskirts of Chestnut Hollow. We see the living room, stage level. The windows are boarded. Stage left is a crumbling fireplace. On the stage right side of the fireplace the letters "L.S." are written on the wall in a scarlet-brown color. Near the fireplace is an old sofa covered with a sheet. Stage right there is an old desk and a chair, also covered with a sheet. There is a door stage left that leads to a back porch and a door stage right that leads to a hallway. Upstage center is an archway that leads to a dining room where a large table sits. There is a door upstage left of the table that leads to the kitchen. The walls are covered with framed religious art of the protestant variety. On the second floor [raised platforms] we can see two bedrooms and a small attic. Each bedroom has a door that leads to an unseen hallway. There is no furniture in the bedrooms. In the attic are dress dummies wearing wedding dresses and a trunk. There is a newer looking card table stage right of center with some folding chairs. The house is lit with scoop lights attached on poles. The extension cords snake all over the rooms.*)

(*AT RISE: It is October, 1978. Friday, near dusk.* **MIRANDA** *appears in the attic area and slowly walks around looking at everything.* **WILMA** *enters center and sits at the desk stage right. She begins to read a book.* **INGRID** *enters and sits in the chair, center. She begins to write in a diary.* **HOLLY** *enters stage left and sits on the chair near the fireplace. She carries a sewing basket and pretends to knit.* **MIRANDA** *exits the attic.*)

HOLLY. Would you both like some tea?

INGRID. Yes.

WILMA. I suppose so.

    (**HOLLY** *rises and exits to kitchen.* **INGRID** *watches her go.* **INGRID** *crosses center archway and retrieves an axe from behind the drapes. She crosses to* **WILMA.** *She clears her throat.*)

What, now?

    (**WILMA** *slowly turns to her.* **INGRID** *begins to hit her with the axe.* **WILMA** *falls off her chair as* **INGRID** *continues to hit her.*)

HOLLY. *(off)* What was that?

INGRID. *(stopping)* I dropped my book.

HOLLY. *(off)* Oh. I'll be right in with the tea.

INGRID. Take your time.

    (*She continues to hit* **WILMA** *with the axe. She stops. She drops the axe.* **HOLLY** *enters. Seeing* **WILMA** *on the floor, she screams and drops the tea things.*)

HOLLY. Oh, Lenora, what have you done?

INGRID. What I had to do.

    (*She whirls on* **HOLLY** *and grabbing a pair of scissors, from her sewing basket, she begins to stab her with the scissors.* **HOLLY** *backs up against the fireplace and cowers on the floor.* **INGRID** *continues to stab her until she stops moving. Taking a last look at both her victims, she exits.* **HOLLY** *reaches her hand up and traces the "L.S." with her finger. Her arm falls and she lies motionless.*)

    (*rushing back into the room*) Well? What do you think?

WILMA. *(sitting up)* It does explain how they were both murdered at the same time.

HOLLY. *(getting up)* I don't know. The kitchen is just down the hall. I think Mrs. Stark would come running in when she heard Lenora bashing her husband's skull in with an axe.

INGRID. Maybe she did. Or maybe Lenora waited until Mrs. Stark went upstairs to the bathroom. That would give her time to dispatch the old man and she could be hiding here, waiting for Mrs. Stark to return to the room. And when Mrs. Stark returns to the room, Lenora pounces!

(She demonstrates with the scissors. **MIRANDA** *enters at the same time, nearly getting stabbed.)*

Oh, sorry.

MIRANDA. That would have hurt. What's going on?

INGRID. We're just acting out…

HOLLY. Sssssh. Don't say anything. Miranda doesn't want to hear about anything that happened in this house. Miranda, you've had a chance to walk around the house. What are your initial impressions?

MIRANDA. The air here is thick. Stagnant, like the bottom of a lake. It's hard to breathe. There is a great deal of sorrow here. And rage. A lot of rage. Fear is here as well. There has been much blood shed in this house. Too much. I smell it. The blood, the fear, the rage, the sorrow. It is all connected somehow to one source. That one source is a kind of energy that still lives here. The energy is blackness and cold. It is deliberately evil. Now, tell me what: happened here.

HOLLY. Thirteen years ago, in 1965, Lenora Stark, 22 year-old librarian and Sunday school teacher, brutally butchered her parents on a sunny, Autumn afternoon. Her father was the Rev. Stark of the local Church of God; he was found on the floor near his desk. He had been struck so many times, he was decapitated. Mrs. Stark was found over here, with a pair of scissors in her throat. Before she died she wrote her daughters initials "L.S." on the wall in her own blood.

WILMA. I've got this new blood recipe I'm dying to try out.

HOLLY. Wilma, I told you, we're keeping the gore to a minimum.

WILMA. I know, but it's a grisly double murder, we got to have some blood.

INGRID. Later that night, the bell in her father's church began to ring wildly. The people of the town came running to see what was the matter. When they climbed the steps to the bell tower, they were greeted by the sight of Lenora, covered in blood, ringing the church bell. She was screaming that her parents had been murdered. Later, when she was asked how was it that she was covered with blood, Lenora said she tried to revive her parents. In her state of shock, she must have carried her father's severed head along with her to the church, because the head sat at her feet, eyes staring up at the bell tower.

MIRANDA. Aren't parsonages usually right next to the church they serve?

INGRID. Not always. Rev. Stark chose this remote location, ten miles from town and the church. He didn't even want neighbors.

MIRANDA. Where is Lenora Stark now?

HOLLY. Upstate, about one hundred miles from here at the asylum for the criminally insane. Maximum security.

MIRANDA. What else?

HOLLY. Lenora's boyfriend, Anthony, broke in here about six months ago, right after Lenora's parole was denied, and shot himself in the attic.

MIRANDA. Shot himself? Are they sure?

HOLLY. According to the Sheriff. It's pretty open and shut. Anthony was still holding the gun when they found his body. The sheriff has found no evidence of foul play.

MIRANDA. Normally when I enter the site of a suicide the overwhelming sensation is utter sadness. What I felt in the attic was fear.

HOLLY. It was Anthony's suicide that prompted Chestnut Hollow to condemn this house and order the owner to tear it down. That's why they are demolishing this place on Monday morning and we've got just this weekend to find out whatever we can.

(**WILMA** *begins to snap photos of the room with a Polaroid.*)

WILMA. I like all the religious art. Creepy. I can cover the set with it. Maybe we can take some of it with us.

THURMIN. *(enters from kitchen)* An outhouse? We have to use an outhouse? When were you going to tell me about that?

HOLLY. Mrs. Thurmin, the house has been abandoned for over 13 years. There is no electricity or plumbing. That's why we brought the generator. Think of it as camping.

THURMIN. I hate camping. The sacrifices I make for my church.

HOLLY. Why did the church insist on representation this weekend? This house is being torn down Monday, what harm could we do?

THURMIN. It's an insurance requirement. In case something happens. As secretary, Pastor Black chose me to go. The only benefit is now Pastor owes me, and I'm going to use this to get our bell choir some new bells.

INGRID. You were secretary when Rev. Stark was pastor, weren't you?

THURMIN. Yes, I was. That's another reason Pastor Black insisted I come. He wants me to put-in a good word on Rev. Stark's behalf.

HOLLY. Is there a good word to put in?

THURMIN. Of course there is. Rev. Stark was a very devout man. He did wonderful things for the church. What happened here was a tragedy. Nothing more. You seem like a bright young lady, why would you pick this story to write a play about?

HOLLY. It's my master's project. I have to write a play and produce it. The play opens at the university in six weeks.

THURMIN. You couldn't write a musical or a comedy? Why dwell on all this...sorrow?

HOLLY. When I was little, one of the foster families I stayed with had a book on crimes and criminals. I remember seeing the photos of the Stark murders for the first time. So horrifying. I couldn't stop looking at the photos. I hid the book under my pillow. I started having nightmares. I still have them occasionally…

WILMA. That reminds me. I can't find that book anywhere. I got two book stores searching. No one's ever heard of it. It's like the book doesn't exist.

HOLLY. *(picks up a envelope)* These photos still have the same impact on me. I have to figure out what happened here. Maybe then this story won't have the power over me that it does. That's why I picked this subject for my play.

THURMIN. Where did you get these crime scene photos?

HOLLY. Sheriff Watkins got them for me. I have to return them to him Sunday.

THURMIN. Do keep in mind that the Starks were real people. The murders destroyed our church. Most people went to other congregations. A few of us moved to the southside of Buffalo which is where the next closest Church of God is.

HOLLY. My play speculates on what happened before the murders. In fact, I am not convinced that Lenora committed the murders.

THURMIN. Don't tell me you're falling for Lenora's story about Abigale? There is no proof of her existing.

MIRANDA. Who's Abigale?

(**GRETCHEN** *enters the room and moves quietly from one painting to another, studying the art.*)

GRETCHEN. Don't mind me.

WILMA. According to Lenora, Abigale is Rev. Stark' s illegitimate daughter who was kept hidden in the barn for the first 12 years of her life. Lenora claims Abigale tunneled out of the barn, killed her parents, and set fire to the barn to cover her tracks, thus framing Lenora for the crimes.

MIRANDA. A twelve year-old girl committed these murders?

WILMA. According to Lenora.

THURMIN. There was not one person who could corroborate that ridiculous story. How do you hide a child for 12 years?

MIRANDA. If this love-child existed, why would Mrs. Stark go along with hiding her?

INGRID. You'd be surprised the length that some women will go to, to hold their family together. A Rebecca Stuart showed up in town one day and came to the church for help. Right?

THURMIN. Yes. I remember her. She was in Chestnut Hollow for almost a year. A mousey little nothing. She became the janitor of the church. One day she tells us she's going back home to Chicago, and she leaves. That's all there is to it.

WILMA. What Lenora claims is that Rev. Stark faked Rebecca's exit and took her into the parsonage because she was pregnant. Lenora said she heard them arguing, and Rebecca was going to tell everyone at the church who the father was. So she hid out at the house during her pregnancy. Something went wrong. Rebecca died during the birth. The Starks were stuck with the baby. Lenora says it was Mrs. Stark who insisted the baby stay with them, and Rev. Stark who insisted the child could never be seen.

MIRANDA. Should have been easy enough to find Rebecca's body, if there was one.

INGRID. They looked. Dug up the whole property. It was even suggested that Rev. Stark may have snuck the body into the bottom of a coffin. They checked the bodies he buried during that time. No luck. They searched high and low for a Rebecca Stuart in Chicago and found nothing.

THURMIN. I'm pretty sure it was a fake name.

GRETCHEN. Sounds fake.

THURMIN. I mean, if the woman didn't want her family to track her, all she had to do was change her name.

HOLLY. Mrs. Thurmin, you knew the Rev. Stark. Is it conceivable to you that he would get involved with this Rebecca?

THURMIN. No. Not him. Not possible.

WILMA. Well, he was a man.

(**GRETCHEN** *laughs out loud.*)

THURMIN. A man of God.

WILMA. Well, even men of God, occasionally stray. Ever read from the old testament?

THURMIN. That was not his nature, and I can tell you how I know for certain. As church secretary, we spent many hours alone together and I never once sensed any inappropriate attention from him.

WILMA. Oh, well. Hard to argue with that.

GRETCHEN. *(standing in front of a painting)* Get a load of this: "Some say the world will end in fire, some say in ice. From what I've tasted of desire, I hold with those who favor fire." What book of the Bible is that from?

MIRANDA. It's not from the Bible. It's Robert Frost, actually.

GRETCHEN. Oh. He sure could turn a phrase when he wanted to.

THURMIN. Tell me, Holly, you seem to know everything there is to know about the story. Why are you here? Surely you don't really expect to uncover any new evidence?

HOLLY. As I said, my play opens in six weeks, and I haven't got an ending I like. It's not enough to recount the murders, it has to add up to something. It has to mean something. It's why there are no successful plays about Jack The Ripper or Lizzie Borden. The audience wants a resolution before the final curtain. Not to mention my lead actress and I don't see eye to eye on the character of Lenora Stark.

INGRID. Hey, Holly, that's not fair. I want to do the best job I can for you.

HOLLY. I know you do.

INGRID. The only way I can portray Lenora Stark properly is if we can decide did she or didn't she? By the end of the weekend I have a feeling I'll be closer to my answer, and you'll figure out your ending. And of course, the show will go on.

WILMA. I'm designing and building the set.

THURMIN. Thank you for sharing.

WILMA. You probably think that building a set is a man's job.

THURMIN. I haven't really given it that much thought.

WILMA. Well, women build sets, too.

HOLLY. Anyway, that's why we're here.

THURMIN. One last question. The church has refused every single request to gain access to this house. How did you manage it?

HOLLY. I met Rev. Black in a foster program growing up. He remembered me, and I convinced him how important this was to me.

(There is a loud electronic squawk and everyone jumps. **HOLLY** *picks up the walkie-talkie.)*

I forgot the Sheriff gave me this. Hello?

SHERIFF WATKINS. Hey, Holly. You ladies settled in for the night?

HOLLY. Yep. Wilma got the generator set up and it's running. We're all set.

WILMA. *(to* **THURMIN***)* Piece of cake.

SHERIFF WATKINS. Good. You contact me if you need anything.

HOLLY. Will do.

SHERIFF WATKINS. You ladies are ten miles from civilization in an abandoned old house. Old houses like the Stark house are liable to creak and groan and make all kinds of noises in the night. Don't let your imaginations run away with you.

WILMA. He wouldn't say that to us if we were men.

SHERIFF WATKINS. What's that?

HOLLY. Nothing, Sheriff. We're good.

SHERIFF WATKINS. One other thing. There's a pretty bad storm heading our way.

HOLLY. I heard. We got a transistor to keep track of the weather.

SHERIFF WATKINS. Okay then. You ladies take care. Over and out.

HOLLY. Over and out.

GRETCHEN. Anybody else hungry? I'm starving.

HOLLY. Come to think of it, I'm hungry too. Let's go into the kitchen and rustle up something good to eat.

THURMIN. I've got everything all laid out and ready to go.

HOLLY. Thank you, Mrs. Thurmin. That was nice of you.

THURMIN. I've got to do something to kill the time.

*(The ladies exit. **MIRANDA** stays on alone. She walks around the room. She picks up one of the crime scene photos. As she slides her fingers across the photo, she seems to be experiencing the murders first hand. Suddenly there is a scream from the other room. She drops the photo.)*

Scene Two

(*SETTING: The same.*)

(*AT RISE: It is close to midnight. We can hear rain.* **GRETCHEN** *is standing by the fireplace listening to the transistor radio.* **INGRID** *and* **WILMA** *are taking measurements of the room.* **MIRANDA** *is studying the crime photos at the card table.* **HOLLY** *and* **MRS. THURMIN** *enter from the kitchen carrying flashlights.*)

HOLLY. Everybody ready to take one last trip to the outhouse?

INGRID. Yeah, let's go. Before it starts raining harder.

GRETCHEN. Wait. Wait. This is that song where you can hear this woman being murdered.

WILMA. What?

GRETCHEN. It's true. They were recording in this cheap studio and a woman was murdered next door during the recording. You can hear her scream. You can hear her die on this record. Ssssh. Listen, here it comes.

(*She turns up the radio. Here is a loud scream.*)

THURMIN. That's gruesome. Change the station.

WILMA. On that happy note, let's all go to the outhouse.

GRETCHEN. You know what? I don't need to go. I'll stay here and hold down the fort.

WILMA. Gretchen, are you sure you can make it through the night?

GRETCHEN. I'm good. I just went a little while ago.

HOLLY. Okay. We'll be right back.

GRETCHEN. I'll be here.

WILMA. And Ingrid, if you happen to see another spider, make sure you shriek into my left ear as my right ear is already deaf.

INGRID. I can't help it. I hate spiders.

WILMA. Be a man.

(The women exit out the backdoor. GRETCHEN exits in the stage right hallway. She appears in the bedroom upper stage left and begins going through the belongings. She finds cash in some of the backpacks and takes it. She exits. MRS. THURMIN enters from the back door. Seeing that no one is in the room, she crosses to the desk and rifles through the drawers looking for something. Meanwhile, GRETCHEN appears in the other bedroom and once again goes through the others' belongings. She pockets some more cash. The rest of the women enter.)

WILMA. Gretchen? Gretchen? I wonder where she is?

HOLLY. She probably went up to bed. I suggest we turn out these lights to save wear on the generator and go up to bed. It's after midnight.

MIRANDA. It sounds like a good idea. Good night.

*(**WILMA** begins to turn the scoop lights off.)*

INGRID. Good night. Sleep tight.

HOLLY. Pleasant dreams.

MIRANDA. Don't count on it.

(The women quickly exit.)

WILMA. *(Not realizing she is alone, she goes about the room clicking off the scoop lights.)* You guys just hang out a minute while I get the lights. It's not that I'm afraid to be by myself in this house, because that's not really it. As a rule, I don't mind being alone in familiar surroundings. But in a strange place, and let's face it, this place is strange, it's nicer to have company. Wouldn't you agree?

(She turns.)

Guys? Guys? When I get up there, I'm going to kill you!

*(She runs off. **GRETCHEN** straightens everyones belongings and quickly lies down on her sleeping bag. The women enter the bedrooms one by one. In the stage right bedroom, **GRETCHEN**, **HOLLY**, **INGRID**. In the stage left bedroom, **THURMIN**, **MIRANDA** and **WILMA**.)*

HOLLY. *(entering)* There you are.

GRETCHEN. I got tired.

(All the women get into their sleeping bags.)

INGRID. This is kind of fun. It's been years since I've been to a slumber party.

GRETCHEN. As long as you don't consider that we're sleeping in an abandoned house where God knows how many murders have been committed, then yeah, you're right, it is fun.

INGRID. I didn't say it was perfect.

THURMIN. Would I offend anyone if I said my prayers?

WILMA. Not me. I pray. Not a lot, but I do pray.

THURMIN. And you?

MIRANDA. Why would you think I would be offended if you prayed?

THURMIN. Well, you do dabble in the dark arts. I don't want to make you uncomfortable.

MIRANDA. What you call dabbling in the dark arts, I call using the talent that God has given me.

THURMIN. If you say so. If you don't mind, I'll start now.

MIRANDA. Please do. Say hello from me.

GRETCHEN. What's with the uptight old broad? It's like she has a pickle up her butt.

HOLLY. She's pretty rigid. I'm still trying to figure out what she's doing here.

GRETCHEN. To make sure you don't find any evidence. If you ask me, she was having an affair with the preacher man.

HOLLY. You think so?

GRETCHEN. Oh, yeah. I can tell. She's still carrying the torch.

INGRID. She sure is acting suspiciously. I would be careful not to let Mrs. Thurmin cloud your judgement.

HOLLY. Not to worry. I actually welcome her input. She has direct knowledge of all the major players in this drama.

INGRID. Just take it with a grain of salt, that's all I'm saying.

HOLLY. How about two grains of salt?

INGRID. Okay, but no more than three.

HOLLY. You got a deal.

THURMIN. Amen. That reminds me. What would ever possess Holly to pick up that hitchhiker?

WILMA. I don't know. We came around the corner and there she was standing right in the middle of the road. We're lucky we didn't kill her.

THURMIN. How convenient that she should be standing there in the road, waiting for us. I think she's one of those motorcycle people. She smells funny. And by funny, I mean bad. It's more than just the B.O. that one comes to expect from street people.

HOLLY. What's that smell?

INGRID. I don't know.

GRETCHEN. I don't smell anything.

THURMIN. It's anybody's guess how many diseases she may be hosting. I'm going to do my best not to let her touch me. I don't trust her.

MIRANDA. Well, she was stranded. And with the storm coming. We couldn't rightly leave her standing on the side of the road in the dark.

THURMIN. She's hiding something. Notice the way she keeps sneaking around the house? Almost like she knows the layout. Wilma, what do you think?

WILMA. She's different, alright. I can't quite read her.

THURMIN. That's my point. What about you, Miranda? Getting any strange vibes or whatever it is you people get?

MIRANDA. She's not what she appears. She bears watching, that I'll agree to. More than that, I can't say.

HOLLY. Gretchen, how did you end-up all alone on the side of the road?

GRETCHEN. My old man kicked me off the back of his bike. I should have seen it coming. There was this skanky blonde at the bar we were at. Huge rack, real slutty. Just his type. Sure enough, half hour later, he goes riding past with the skanky slut on the back. I picked up a big rock and threw it, but they were already over the hill. She better hope I never run into her again.

INGRID. What will you do now?

GRETCHEN. I'm heading up to Rhode Island where I have family.

INGRID. Rhode Island is nice.

GRETCHEN. Once this rain stops, all I will have to trouble you for is a ride to the Greyhound station.

HOLLY. No, trouble. Gretchen, you're new to this story. What is your take on it?

GRETCHEN. Well, when you first told me what happened, I thought that Lenora and her boyfriend did it. That was my best guess until you told me that the boyfriend killed himself here six months ago. Now I'm not so sure.

INGRID. Isn't it possible that the guilt became too much for him and he would come here and take his own life?

GRETCHEN. If he hung himself, I'd say maybe. That would seem like a punishment he might pick for himself. Especially right after Lenora's parole was denied. But to shoot himself in the head? Let me see that photo again.

(**HOLLY** *passes her a photo.*)

Yeah. Look at him lying there. It seems staged to me.

HOLLY. How so?

GRETCHEN. If I was going to shoot myself in the head, I'd put the gun here.

(*She indicates under her chin.*)

And Bang!

(*She slams her hand on the floor.*)

THURMIN. What was that?

MIRANDA. I didn't hear anything.

GRETCHEN. I'd take my head off with no chance of missing. Or a lot of people take the barrel of the gun into their mouth. Bang!

(Again she slams her hand on the floor.)

THURMIN. There it goes again.

WILMA. I didn't hear anything.

GRETCHEN. But this guy, puts the gun above his right ear and fires.

(She demonstrates and falls down on her sleeping bag.)

Look at his hand holding the gun. Neat and straight next to his body. I shoot myself and I fall.

(She demonstrates.)

What are the odds that my arm lands perfectly by the side of my body? Still holding the gun? It's staged. I'm telling you.

HOLLY. *(taking the photo back)* I never noticed that before, but you're right. Oh, my God. If he was murdered… it couldn't have been Lenora, she's been locked-up in the asylum. Who would have reason to kill him?

INGRID. Someone with something to hide.

GRETCHEN. The bigger issue of course is the fact that if he was murdered, he was murdered prowling around this house, possibly looking for clues. Isn't that what you all are doing here?

HOLLY. What are you saying?

GRETCHEN. I should have held out for a trucker. Five chicks in a van, I knew that was bad luck.

(She rolls over on her sleeping bag. **HOLLY** *and* **INGRID** *just look at each other.)*

WILMA. Everybody ready for me to get the light?

THURMIN. Is the door locked?

INGRID. Is the door locked?

WILMA. I'll check.

HOLLY. Let me check.

>*(The women lock the doors.)*

>It's locked now.

INGRID. Good.

WILMA. It's locked now.

THURMIN. Good.

GRETCHEN. Good.

HOLLY. I'll get the light. Everyone got her flashlight?

WILMA. Light going out. Everyone got their flashlight?

>*(She clicks the light off.)*

HOLLY. Here goes.

>*(She clicks the light off.)*

>*(Silence in the house. Thunder shakes the house.)*

GRETCHEN. Here comes the storm.

INGRID. I keep hearing that scream from the radio.

HOLLY. Shut up. I'm trying not to think about it.

WILMA. You think that woman was really murdered on that record?

THURMIN. Stop it. I'm trying to get that scream out of my head.

MIRANDA. Nobody will sleep tonight.

GRETCHEN. I can't sleep.

>*(One by one the women turn on their flashlights.)*

>*(blackout)*

Scene Three

(SETTING: The same.)

(AT RISE: The next afternoon. **WILMA** *is tending a fire in the fireplace.* **MIRANDA** *is sitting in the attic in front of a lit candle and appears to be in a trance. There is a jack-o-lantern on the dining room table with a lit candle in it.)*

GRETCHEN. *(enters)* Ah, a fire. Way to go. It's so cold in here.

WILMA. This ought to help.

(They both warm themselves by the fire.)

GRETCHEN. Did you carve the jack-o-lantern, too?

WILMA. Yeah. Halloween is Tuesday.

GRETCHEN. Yep. It's my favorite holiday.

WILMA. Mine, too.

(pause)

Ingrid told me what your old man did to you. That's brutal. I hope he rots in Hell.

GRETCHEN. Hell won't have him. I guess I should have seen it comin'. I got family in Delaware I can stay with for awhile.

WILMA. That's good anyway.

GRETCHEN. Yeah.

WILMA. Men. What are they good for?

GRETCHEN. Nothing. Well, I guess I can think of one thing.

WILMA. Yeah. Some of them are good at it.

(They laugh.)

THURMIN. *(enters)* Mind if I share your fire?

WILMA. Not at all.

THURMIN. Dld either of you hear noises in the attic last night?

GRETCHEN. What kind of noises?

THURMIN. It was a squeaking sound. It sounded to me like someone was rocking in that old rocking chair up there.

WILMA. I didn't hear anything.

GRETCHEN. Me either.

(*THURMIN sits and taking a piece of fabric from her sewing basket, begins to cut out a pattern with a big pair of silver scissors. The others look at her.*)

THURMIN. We're making new costumes for the nativity. I've got to cut all the patterns out by Monday.

(*She continues.* **INGRID** *and* **HOLLY** *enter.*)

INGRID. I'm not feeling sorry for myself, and I'm not trying to back out. All I'm saying is that I've never struggled so much with a role in my whole life. I've been having nightmares every night. I open my eyes and Lenora Stark is standing at the foot of my bed.

HOLLY. Really?

INGRID. Yes. She talks to me. Over and over, she says it's her fault but she didn't do it. What the hell does that mean? The problem goes right to the root of her character. If Lenora is a cold-blooded killer, that changes her value system. I am trying to build a believable character. Is she the Sunday school teacher or is she the axe murderer?

HOLLY. She may be both.

INGRID. I can't do both.

HOLLY. Sure you can.

INGRID. She can't be both and be sane.

WILMA. She's in a nut house. I'm just saying.

HOLLY. Okay. This is getting us nowhere. You know what would really help me? If each one of you told me what you think happened here. I would greatly appreciate that. Who wants to go first?

THURMIN. Allow me. As we know, the killer supposedly entered from the kitchen with an axe. Rev. Stark was working at his desk, right over there. Mrs. Stark was sitting right about where I am. Now, the coroner could not determine who was killed first. Rev. Stark was struck 29 times while his wife was stabbed with a pair of scissors. My question is, no matter who the killer decides to strike first, what was the other one doing? They both had defensive wounds on their arms and hands, which rules out drugging them first.

HOLLY. What's your solution?

THURMIN. Two killers. Lenora and Anthony. They entered together and attacked at the same time.

INGRID. Who killed who?

THURMIN. Anthony killed Rev. Stark and Lenora killed her mother. They thought they would get away with it until Mrs. Stark wrote her killer's initials on the wall in her own blood. Talk about the writing on the wall. That's what convinced me and that's what convinced the jury. Too bad she didn't implicate Anthony. He got away with it for 13 years until she was denied parole. The way I hear it, the pressure was too much for him and he lost his mind.

INGRID. And the motivation?

THURMIN. They had two powerful motivations. The Starks didn't approve of Anthony and forbid him to marry their daughter. He was Catholic.

WILMA. What's wrong with Catholics?

THURMIN. Nothing is wrong with them, but if you're a protestant minister's daughter in 1965, you don't marry one. Not to mention, the Starks were very well-off. Mrs. Stark had a great deal of money when she came to the marriage. Lenora was their sole heir. Getting the Starks out of the way would allow them to marry and be set for life.

GRETCHEN. I don't think so. Things are almost never what they appear to be. I say it went-down like this: Mrs. Stark returns home unexpectedly and catches her preacher man in a clinch with his secret lover. Mrs. Stark goes a little berserk, grabs the axe and bashes the padre's brains in. But Mrs. Stark is not finished. It is not enough to punish just one of the sinners. Mrs. Stark turns her rage on the other woman. But this other woman will not go down without a fight.

(grabbing the scissors from **THURMIN***)*

She grabs a pair of scissors and manages to drive them into Mrs. Stark's throat. Two corpses, two killers, one survivor. On her way out the door, the secret lover writes "L.S." on the wall over the bloody body of Mrs. Stark, thereby condemning Lenora for both murders.

(pause)

What we have here is a love triangle that turned deadly. Happens all the time. The fact that Anthony was murdered in the attic while looking for clues tells me that the triangle's only surviving member thinks there is still incriminating evidence here. And the kicker is, by killing Anthony and getting the dump condemned, she's going to get away with murder again. Whoever she is, she's smart. And very, very dangerous.

(She hands **THURMIN** *her scissors back.)*

HOLLY. Thank you, Gretchen. That actually makes a lot of sense to me. Wilma, what's your conclusion?

WILMA. *(rises and crosses behind sofa)* Lenora didn't do it. If she was truly in love, they would have just run away. Anthony had no part in it. Why would he stick around for 13 years waiting for Leonora to get out? And then after she is denied parole he kills himself? No, to me, that points to the fact that they are both innocent. And Lenora's story about a secret love child hidden in the barn, who got out and killed them and disappeared? Too incredible. And have you really looked at the crime photos? No way a 12 year-old kid did that.

HOLLY. *(sitting on sofa)* Then who did it?

WILMA. No one we know. No one we suspect.

INGRID. Some crazy just passing by?

WILMA. No. Someone in town. Someone who knew the family's routines.

HOLLY. And the motive?

WILMA. Just for the fun of it.

HOLLY. A thrill kill?

WILMA. Yeah, a thrill kill. I like that. We've all imagined what it would be like to murder someone. Not someone we're angry with, necessarily. But a stranger. Just to see what it was like. To see what it was like to actually go through with it. To see what the expression of the victim would be. To see what it would feel like to take an axe to someone's head. Or to drive a sharp pair of scissors into someone's throat. What would that sound like? What would their last words be? Would they beg for their lives?

(pause)

We've all imagined these things, but most of us would never actually go through with it. Because thinking about it and maybe actually even planning it out would be enough. But not for everyone. For some this notion begins to consume their every waking moment and even their dreams. They become convinced that they must follow through or die. Maybe it was someone who picked a family name out of a phone book. They came in, butchered the Rev. and Mrs. Stark and disappeared back into the fabric of life. For some once is enough. They are satisfied to play the kill over and over again in their minds and that is enough to control that powerful urge. But for others it is only the beginning. The first taste of blood. We're never going to know who killed the Starks.

THURMIN. I want to switch bedrooms.

HOLLY. That's certainly is a fresh perspective on the murders. Thank you for sharing. I agree that Lenora didn't do it. I believe she did have a step-sister named Abigale. Think about it. What if it did happen that way? What if Rev. Stark did get a woman pregnant? He invites her into his remote home until the baby is born. But something goes wrong. The mother dies in childbirth. They bury the body and raise a secret child. Of course she can't be seen. Someone might see a resemblance to either parent. How would they explain her? So they keep all visitors away and raise Abigale as a secret. Little by little Abigale finds out what is happening to her. Can you imagine what that feels like? Living like a prisoner. And to make matters much worse, Lenora testified that her father had been molesting her for years, and she was pretty sure had been molesting Abigale.

THURMIN. That's absurd. When Lenora came up with that I knew she was just grasping at straws. She would have said anything to stay out of jail.

HOLLY. We can't be sure. What if it were true? Can you even imagine the rage that could build up in a child? She somehow escapes, kills the Starks and implicates Lenora. Had Lenora been home at the time of the murders I am sure there would have been three corpses. To seal Lenora's fate, Abigale gets rid of all the proof that she ever existed, by burning the barn and disappearing.

THURMIN. What about the blood on the wall? How does that get there?

HOLLY. Abigale wrote it.

THURMIN. And you're telling me a 12 year-old would be capable of all this?

HOLLY. Yes.

WILMA. How old would she be now?

GRETCHEN. Twenty-five.

(**MIRANDA** *blows out her candle and exits the attic.*)

HOLLY. Yes, twenty-five.

WILMA. Where is she now?

HOLLY. Close. I think she watches this house. Anthony comes in looking for evidence and she kills him. I'm thinking that's more and more a possibility.

INGRID. And here's where my revelation comes in. I just had it last night. My new theory is Lenora did it but she doesn't know she did it.

WILMA. How is that even possible?

INGRID. Hear me out. Let's say Lenora was being molested. Children who have been molested over a long period of time, sometimes develop other personalities. That way, it is someone else who is being violated. So, Lenora creates Abigale. It's Abigale who is the victim, Abigale who is a prisoner in the Stark's house. Over the years, she became so good at becoming Abigale when she needed to, that Abigale became a real person to her. And when her parents refused to let her marry Anthony it was Abigale who lashed out and killed them. There's the ending you have been looking for, Holly. Picture this! Lenora in prison, in front of a mirror, combing her hair and she begins to cry out. "There she is! She's here! It's Abigale!" And she points right into the mirror. It was Leonora who killed her parents, only she doesn't know she did it. Because she was Abigale when she killed them. It solves everything!

HOLLY. Abigale and Lenora are the same person, So all the bad things that happened to Lenora, happened to Abigale and not her. And when it came time to punish her tormentors it was Abigale who wielded the axe.

INGRID. Exactly.

HOLLY. You know, you may be on to something.

INGRID. Oh, I'm on to something.

(**MIRANDA** *enters.*)

HOLLY. Miranda, what's the matter?

MIRANDA. I keep having this vision of Lenora standing in that doorway covered in blood.

HOLLY. Do you think you are seeing the actual murder?

MIRANDA. No, it's clearly a vision of something that will happen in the future.

INGRID. The future? How can you be so sure?

MIRANDA. I see that boarded up window, that crumbling fire place, that card table.

WILMA. This house will be gone Monday by noon. The only future this house has is tonight and tomorrow. And we are here tonight and tomorrow.

MIRANDA. Exactly. But that isn't all I see.

HOLLY. What else did you see?

MIRANDA. I see a pair of bloody hands in front of my face.

HOLLY. Bloody hands? Do you have any idea whose hands they are?

MIRANDA. I know exactly whose hands they are.

GRETCHEN. Whose?

MIRANDA. Mine.

(They turn to look at her. **THURMIN** *drops her scissors on the floor.)*

(blackout)

Scene Four

(*SETTING: The same.*)

(*AT RISE: Saturday night. A few hours later. A thunderstorm is raging.* **GRETCHEN** *and* **MIRANDA** *are sitting by the fireplace.* **MIRANDA** *is giving* **GRETCHEN** *a reading with Tarot cards.* **HOLLY** *is sitting at the card table studying the crime scene photos. The transistor radio is on, and music is playing quietly in the background.*)

HOLLY. (*rises*) I'm getting more coffee. Anybody want some?

MIRANDA. I'm good.

GRETCHEN. No, thanks. My last cup tasted funny.

(*She exits.*)

You nailed my past and you nailed my present. The things you know about me just blows my mind!

MIRANDA. It's not me, it's the cards. I'm just reading what they're revealing to you.

GRETCHEN. Well, it's freaking' me out a little.

MIRANDA. Should I stop?

GRETCHEN. No. I can't stop now. I need to know about my future. Is that these three cards, here?

MIRANDA. That's right. Ready?

GRETCHEN. Go ahead.

(*She flips a card over.*)

The hangman! I knew it! I'm going to die!

MIRANDA. No, no, no. The Hangman means limbo. You are waiting to make up your mind about something. You are waiting to make a judgment about your future. It is often a sign that you should be patient and not rush into anything.

(*She flips the second card.*)

GRETCHEN. The reaper? Don't tell me that doesn't mean death!

MIRANDA. The reaper represents change. A significant change is coming.

GRETCHEN. Being dead after being alive is a pretty significant change.

MIRANDA. It doesn't mean that. You are being way too literal. The Reaper card represents the end of something and the beginning of something else. Often times the thing that is ending is bad and the change or start of something new is positive. Besides it's never the meaning of one card alone but rather the spread and sequence of cards that one must consider. So far, for your future, you are waiting to make a big change. Here's the last card.

(She flips the final card.)

GRETCHEN. A castle. Thank goodness. How bad can the castle be? What does it mean, I'm getting a new house? I'm moving? What?

MIRANDA. Look closer at the card. The tower is being struck by lightning and it's on fire. This card is called The Tower and it means destruction.

GRETCHEN. I knew it. I had this feeling ever since I came into this damn house that I would be going out in a body bag.

MIRANDA. Gretchen, wait. Let me explain.

GRETCHEN. No. Stop. Just stop. I don't want to hear anymore. This was a mistake. I need to…I need…um. I need to get out of this room right now. Okay. I need to get out of this room. All of a sudden I can't breathe. Maybe it's the fire. I don't know.

*(She rushes out, almost knocking over **HOLLY**, as she enters with her cup of coffee.)*

MIRANDA. Gretchen!

HOLLY. What was that all about?

MIRANDA. She's upset about her reading.

HOLLY. Is it that bad?

MIRANDA. Yes. It's the worst possible combination. I've only had those cards come up once before all in a row that way. It was one of my regular clients. The woman burst into tears and ran out of my house. I only saw her one other time after that.

HOLLY. Where did you see her?

MIRANDA. In her coffin.

HOLLY. Is Gretchen's reading really that bad?

MIRANDA. It's deadly. I'd better go find her.

(**MIRANDA** *exits.* **WILMA** *enters from stage left door, soaking wet.*)

WILMA. I think I got a sliver from that outhouse.

HOLLY. Ouch. Where?

WILMA. Where else? My butt. Who makes wooden toilet seats?

HOLLY. Does it hurt?

WILMA. Yeah. I think it's in there pretty deep.

HOLLY. Do you want me to take a look?

WILMA. NO, that's okay.

HOLLY. Oh, thank God. I thought our friendship at least called for an offer.

WILMA. I appreciate the gesture.

(**INGRID** *enters, also soaking wet.*)

INGRID. Hey, where did you go? I was talking to you and when I came out you were gone.

WILMA. I have a sliver in my butt.

INGRID. *(laughing)* Do you really?

WILMA. Hey, it's not funny! It hurts!

HOLLY. You two are soaking wet. I'll get you some towels.

(*She exits.*)

INGRID. Oh, and very funny with the scratching sounds while I was in the outhouse.

WILMA. What are you talking about?

INGRID. Like you don't know. The scratching sounds you were making on the roof of the outhouse to scare me.

WILMA. It wasn't me. I swear. First of all, I got a butt sliver. How am I climbing outhouses?

INGRID. Well, if it wasn't you, then who…

(THURMIN *enters.*)

THURMIN. Has anyone seen my scissors?

INGRID. Those big silver ones?

THURMIN. Yes.

INGRID. I haven't seen them.

WILMA. Me either.

THURMIN. I can't find them.

WILMA. I have a sliver in my butt.

THURMIN. Are you looking for sympathy or trying to warn me?

WILMA. A little from column 'A' and a little from column 'B'.

THURMIN. I see. In that case, I am sorry for you discomfort and I can assure you that no part of my body has now or will ever come into physical contact with an outhouse toilet seat. Ever.

WILMA. Ah, you must've got that levitation thing down where you hover above the seat. I could never manage to do that. I don't have the balance. I just got to take my chances.

(*pause*)

Oh, Ingrid, I love this song! Let's dance!

(WILMA *and* INGRID *begin to dance to the music.*)

THURMIN. I knew it. I just knew it. Everything I've ever heard about you theatre people is coming true right before my eyes.

WILMA. Hey, lighten up. Women have danced together since the beginning of time. Care to join us?

THURMIN. Thanks, but no. The only person I've ever danced with is my dead husband.

WILMA. There's a picture for your scrap book.

THURMIN. Why don't you see if you can get some news about the storm on that thing?

INGRID. Good idea.

(She spins the dial.)

HOLLY. *(enters)* Here's some towels.

WILMA. Thanks.

MIRANDA. *(enters)* Anyone seen Gretchen? I can't find her anywhere.

THURMIN. I haven't seen her since dinner. Have you seen my scissors?

MIRANDA. The big silver ones?

THURMIN. Yes.

MIRANDA. No.

WILMA. I haven't seen Gretchen either.

INGRID. Wait a minute. There's something on the radio about the storm.

RADIO. According to our sources the two women escaped late last night after killing a guard. They are armed and extremely dangerous. The Chestnut Hollow Sheriff's office is advising all citizens to stay inside and lock all doors and windows and report any suspicious activity immediately.

(WILMA crosses to the back door and locks it.)

To repeat, convicted killer Lenora Stark escaped from the state asylum late last night with the aid of fellow inmate Ann Bly. They killed correctional officer Belinda Simmons. They are armed and extremely dangerous. Lenora Stark brutally butchered her parents, the reverend Thomas Stark and his wife Esther Stark, 13 years ago in Chestnut Hollow. Rev. Stark was beheaded with an axe and Mrs. Stark was discovered with a pair of scissors in her throat. The case is also remembered for the bizarre defense offered-up by

Lenora Stark. She claimed that the actual murderer was a 12 year-old prisoner in the Stark home named Abigale who was fathered by Reverend Stark and hidden from the public. All attempts to verify or trace Abigale were not successful. We will bring you updates as they become available. In other news, the storm continues to worsen with flooding reported on the south side of town…

(**INGRID** *clicks off the radio.*)

WILMA. I don't like this.

(*The walkie-talkie makes a loud noise and everyone jumps.*)

SHERIFF WATKINS. (*over walkie-talkie*) Holly? Holly? Come in. Do you copy?

HOLLY. (*picking up walkie-talkie*) Right here, Sheriff.

SHERIFF WATKINS. I got something to tell you, but I don't want you to panic.

HOLLY. We just heard on the radio. She escaped last night, why are we just hearing about it now?

SHERIFF WATKINS. Sometimes they hold back the information in hopes they can quickly retrieve the escapees.

HOLLY. Why would she escape now? Do you think she's heading here?

SHERIFF WATKINS. Very unlikely. It's almost one hundred miles from here. Just to be safe, I've sent Deputy Terry out there to keep an eye on the place.

HOLLY. That makes me feel better. Is it true that Lenora killed a correctional officer?

SHERIFF WATKINS. That's what they're saying. That just makes things worse for her. I'll let you know if I hear anything.

HOLLY. Thanks.

SHERIFF WATKINS. Over and out.

HOLLY. Yeah.

(*She sets the walkie-talkie down.*)

INGRID. I think our ending just changed. I can't believe Lenora killed a prison guard and escaped from the asylum. If she didn't have blood on her hands before, she does now.

HOLLY. Sheriff Watkins says she's most likely not coming here. Why would she?

THURMIN. Not coming here? Of course she's coming here! Do you think it's just a coincidence that she picked this weekend to break out of the asylum? She found out you were going to be here or she found out they're tearing her house down, I am not sure which. One thing I know for sure, she's headed here.

HOLLY. Let's not panic. Even if her intentions are to get here, how could she manage that? To travel one hundred miles in this storm? There's no way she can do it. Miranda, what do you think?

MIRANDA. It's not good. It's not good. She's escaped. She has fresh blood on her hands. I don't like it.

THURMIN. Let's get out of here. I say we hop in that van and drive into town. At least drop me off somewhere.

INGRID. The radio was saying many of the roads are washed out. The south of town is flooded.

THURMIN. I'll take my chances with the flood.

HOLLY. What does everybody else think? Should we get out? Hey, Gretchen's still not here.

WILMA. I'm sure she's in the house somewhere. Gretchen? Gretchen?

(*There is a knock on the outside door. The women react. The knocking gets louder.*)

MIRANDA. Maybe it's Gretchen. She went to the outhouse and we locked her out. That must be it.

HOLLY. (*crossing to door*) This is silly. Who is it?

DEPUTY TERRY. (*off*) Deputy Terry. Sheriff Watkins sent me.

HOLLY. It's the deputy!

(**HOLLY** *unlocks the door and opens it.*)

DEPUTY TERRY. *(enters)* Ladies. I'm Deputy Terry.

THURMIN. I was expecting a male.

DEPUTY TERRY. So was my father. He got over it. So will you. Is everyone alright?

HOLLY. We're fine. One of us is missing. Her name is Gretchen. She's a hitchhiker we picked up.

DEPUTY TERRY. A hitchhiker? You picked up a hitchhiker?

HOLLY. Yes.

DEPUTY TERRY. It's never a good idea to pick up hitchhikers.

HOLLY. Be that as it may, she's still missing!

THURMIN. We can look for her on our way out. Deputy Terry, help us get our things to the van so we can get out of here.

DEPUTY TERRY. All four tires on the van are slashed.

HOLLY. Slashed? By who?

DEPUTY TERRY. I have no way of knowing. I just got here. There's no way that van out there is going anywhere.

THURMIN. Then let's go in your squad car. We need to get out of here right away. The slashed tires are proof of that.

DEPUTY TERRY. My patrol car is stuck in the ditch, down the road a bit. There's no way we're getting out. No, I'm afraid the best thing to do is stay put till the storm dies down.

(There is a blood-curdling scream. **DEPUTY TERRY** *jumps. She pulls out her revolver.)*

What was that? Where did that come from?

HOLLY. It sounds like it came from the kitchen. Right through there.

DEPUTY TERRY. *(drawing her gun)* Everybody stay here.

(She slowly exits.)

HOLLY. Be careful.

DEPUTY TERRY. *(off)* Oh, my God. Oh, my God.

WILMA. What is it?

DEPUTY TERRY. *(enters carrying a bloody towel)* Did Gretchen have a medium build and long dark hair?

INGRID. Yes.

DEPUTY TERRY. I found her.

HOLLY. Where is she?

DEPUTY TERRY. She's dead. Her throat was slit. With these scissors.

INGRID. Oh, my God.

THURMIN. Those are my scissors.

DEPUTY TERRY. Oh?

THURMIN. Yes, but I didn't kill her.

DEPUTY TERRY. No one said you did.

HOLLY. Did you see anyone?

DEPUTY TERRY. No, but now the kitchen door is wide open, and I tried it before I came to this back door. It was locked.

MIRANDA. That means Lenora is here. In this house.

DEPUTY TERRY. Let's not jump to any conclusions. Hand me that walkie-talkie. I'll let the Sheriff know what's going on. I'll take a walk around and secure the place. You all stay here. Together. And scream like hell if you see anything. And nobody touch the body.

THURMIN. Let's make a run for it!

DEPUTY TERRY. Just stay put until I have a look round. We have to make sure it's safe. Then we can decide the best course of action.

(into the walkie-talkie)

Sheriff Watkins. It's Deputy Terry. I'm going to need some back-up out here. There's been a murder…

*(She exits. The women gather around the card table to look at the bloody scissors. **LENORA**, dressed in prison attire and covered in blood, appears in the attic. She falls to her knees and tries to wipe the blood from her hands.)*

(blackout)

End of Act One

ACT II

Scene One

(SETTING: The same.)

(AT RISE: Ten minutes later. **MIRANDA** *and* **MRS. THURMIN** *are huddled near the fire as the* **DEPUTY,** **HOLLY, INGRID,** *and* **WILMA** *carry the body of* **GRETCHEN** *from the kitchen into the stage right hallway. The radio is on.* **LENORA** *is no longer in the attic.)*

RADIO. The body of one of the convicts, Anne Bly, was found in the woods. She had been shot by one of the guards. The search continues for escaped convict Lenora Stark. Chestnut Hollow residents are urged to stay indoors and to keep the doors and windows locked. Lenora Stark is considered armed and extremely dangerous. If anyone has any information about her whereabouts call the Chestnut Hollow Sheriff's office.

*(***MIRANDA*** clicks off the radio.)*

THURMIN. I would feel safer if Deputy Terry was a man.

MIRANDA. Don't let Wilma hear you say that.

THURMIN. I can't help it. It's how I feel.

MIRANDA. I'm just grateful to have help.

THURMIN. I guess.

(The others enter.)

DEPUTY TERRY. We put the…body in the small bedroom off the hall. Until the coroner gets here. Thank you for helping me. In case you're wondering, that was my first body. This is Chestnut Hollow. I never dreamt I'd ever have to do something like that.

WILMA. You're doing a wonderful job, Deputy.

DEPUTY TERRY. Thank you. Sheriff Watkins is aware of our situation and he has alerted the state authorities. Unfortunately the bridge to this side of town was damaged in the storm.

THURMIN. That bridge is our only way back into town!

DEPUTY TERRY. Unless you want to hike through the forest, that is. It's really wicked out there.

HOLLY. Have you seen anything yet?

DEPUTY TERRY. Not yet. Mrs. Thurmin, when was the last time you saw your scissors?

THURMIN. I had them earlier today when I was cutting out patterns. Then I couldn't find them.

DEPUTY TERRY. Where was your sewing basket?

THURMIN. In the kitchen. On the table.

DEPUTY TERRY. So, everyone here had access to them.

THURMIN. Yes, I suppose so. But, we were all in this room when we heard Gretchen scream.

DEPUTY TERRY. That's true. Since I'm the only officer here, with back-up definitely delayed, I think it would be wise if one of you accompanied me as I search the house and property. If nobody wants to I would understand. I sure would appreciate it, though.

HOLLY. I'll come with you.

DEPUTY TERRY. Thank you. I have an extra gun. Who is comfortable handling it?

MIRANDA. I dated a man who taught me how to shoot.

DEPUTY TERRY. You a good shot?

MIRANDA. I'm not bad.

DEPUTY TERRY. Here you go.

(*She hands her a revolver.*)

The safety is on.

MIRANDA. I noticed.

DEPUTY TERRY. If it comes down to saving your own life or someone else's, do you think you could shoot another human being?

MIRANDA. I think so. If I had to.

THURMIN. I don't like just waiting here. I feel like a sitting duck. I'm going to my room and locking my door. The window is boarded and I'm not letting anyone in.

DEPUTY TERRY. Actually, that's not a bad idea. Maybe you all should do that for now.

WILMA. Sounds good to me.

(The women exit. DEPUTY TERRY sits down.)

DEPUTY TERRY. Give me just a minute, will you?

HOLLY. What's the matter?

DEPUTY TERRY. I'm not sure I can do this. I didn't sign up for this. That woman had a pair of scissors sticking out of her throat. The look on her face…

HOLLY. I know. I know. But you can't fall apart. We need you. You're scared, so am I. We're also in danger. Right now, Sheriff Watkins is getting help to us, right?

DEPUTY TERRY. Yes, but in this storm, who knows how long it will take them to get here.

HOLLY. We can't think about that right now. All we have to do is hang in there until help arrives. Okay?

DEPUTY TERRY. Part of me wants to run right out that door.

HOLLY. And I'd be right behind you. But we can't.

DEPUTY TERRY. No, we can't. Okay. Focus. Let's go search and secure the crime scene.

HOLLY. Now you're talking. How do we do that?

DEPUTY TERRY. We search for the killer's whereabouts while at the same time securing the premises.

HOLLY. Let's do it.

(They exit into the kitchen.)

(MIRANDA, WILMA and MRS. THURMIN appear in the bedroom stage left. INGRID appears in her room stage right and locks the door. THURMIN quickly locks the door.)

THURMIN. There. I feel safer here.

MIRANDA. Wait a minute. Holly is with Deputy Terry and Gretchen is dead. That means that Ingrid is all alone in her room.

WILMA. I didn't think of that. Maybe one of us should go to be with her.

(*There is a loud bang.*)

I'm sure she's fine.

MIRANDA. As long as she keeps her door locked and doesn't open it, she should be fine.

WILMA. Yeah.

MIRANDA. As long as we're going to be sitting here, do you mind if I try some automatic writing?

THURMIN. What's that?

MIRANDA. I try and get myself into a trance-like state and I let my subconscious control my writing hand. Most the time I get nothing, but every now and then I'll get a message from the spirit world.

WILMA. What do you hope to achieve?

MIRANDA. I hope to get some information that will shed light on who killed Gretchen. It may save our lives.

WILMA. Is there something I could do to help?

MIRANDA. If you could turn the pages of the sketch book once the page is full, that would be helpful.

WILMA. I can do that.

MIRANDA. Okay, let's begin.

(**MIRANDA** *gets a sketch pad from her suitcase and begins the automatic writing process. At first her hand just rests quietly on the sketch pad. She closes her eyes. Her head droops. Her hand begins to write slowly at first and then faster. There is a knock on Ingrid's door.* **INGRID** *crosses to the door and unlocks it. She slowly opens it.* **LENORA** *quickly enters the room and closing the door, locks it.*)

LENORA. Don't make a sound.

INGRID. I won't. Please, don't hurt me.

LENORA. Hurt you? I won't hurt you.

INGRID. Okay.

LENORA. Do you know who I am?

INGRID. You're Lenora Stark. My name is Ingrid.

LENORA. I know who you are.

INGRID. We have written to each other.

LENORA. Yes.

INGRID. Why are you here?

LENORA. To stop Abigale. She's in this house.

INGRID. Have you seen her?

LENORA. Not yet. But she's here. I begged you not to tell our story. I begged you not to come here. I knew it would enrage Abigale. I knew it would bring her back here to this house.

INGRID. You killed that prison guard.

LENORA. I didn't. I have never killed anyone. It was Annie. I told her not to. She stabbed the guard. Annie was shot. She was able to keep walking for awhile. She was…there was so much blood. She died in the woods. In my arms. I had to leave her there. That way.

INGRID. Then you are still innocent.

LENORA. Not innocent. I was too scared to stop Annie from stabbing the guard. Just like I was too scared to stop my father. I should have done something. I should have protected Abigale. It's hard for people to understand that kind of fear. Part of me was glad that at least it wasn't always me that father was…you know. That's wrong. I know.

INGRID. But to be locked-up all these years when you didn't kill your parents.

LENORA. I've accepted my punishment long ago. Knowing what is right and not doing it is also a sin. I should be punished. I'm here now to stop it. It must stop. No more blood. There has been too much blood. Only I can stop it.

INGRID. Why are you the only one who can stop this?

LENORA. Because I am the only one alive who believes that Abigale exists.

INGRID. Are you sure it's Abigale?

LENORA. Yes. Over the years she has sent me articles to taunt me. She has never stopped killing. Anyone who would hurt her. She killed Anthony. Anthony didn't shoot himself. Anthony had a phobia of guns. He came here looking for evidence that Abigale existed.

(pause)

It's not Abigale's fault. We created her. I tried to care for her. I spent many hours with her every day in her room in the barn. On really cold nights I snuck her into this house, into my bedroom. I read her stories and tucked her into bed every night. I made her believe that she was a princess and that she had to stay in hiding to be safe. I told her one day she could be free. That was going to be how this story ended. I ended every bed time story with "And they both lived…We never said, "Happily ever-after." We were saving that for the day when we were free. We kept each other going for the day we could say, "And they both lived happily ever-after." We never got to say that. I loved Abigale so. I still do.

*(**MIRANDA** stops writing. She begins to come out of her trance. She begins to scan the pages of scribbles for meaning.)*

INGRID. Why did your father do what he did?

LENORA. Father was two people. He was never happy. When he was father he would brood and keep to himself and speak very quietly. When he was the other… he would hurt us. No one must ever discover father's secret. Mother was too weak to fight him. She knew. She knew. We were all prisoners. Now, I have to set Abigale free. No matter what the cost. Will you help me?

INGRID. What can I do?

LENORA. Don't tell the others that you have seen me. Let me find Abigale. If the Deputy takes me away, Abigale will kill you all.

(There is a knock on the door.)

DEPUTY TERRY. Ingrid, you alright in there?

*(**INGRID** opens the door. **LENORA** hides behind the door. **DEPUTY TERRY** and **HOLLY** appear in the open door.)*

INGRID. I'm fine.

DEPUTY TERRY. I thought I heard voices in here.

INGRID. I heard voices, too. I thought it was you guys. The voices were coming from the attic.

DEPUTY TERRY. The attic. We'll go take a look up there and then we'll get everyone together for an update.

INGRID. Okay.

HOLLY. Stay put. I'll be right back.

INGRID. I'm not going anywhere.

DEPUTY TERRY. Now close the door and lock it.

*(**INGRID** closes the door and locks it. **INGRID** and **LENORA** look at one another.)*

LENORA. Thank you.

INGRID. You're welcome.

*(**LENORA** starts to go.)*

You could be lying to me.

LENORA. Yes. And you could be lying to me.

INGRID. I have nothing to gain by lying to you.

LENORA. And I have nothing left to lose.

INGRID. This can't end well.

LENORA. It was never meant to.

*(She quietly exits out the door. **INGRID** locks the door.)*
(pause)
*(**MIRANDA** finds something in the sketch pad.)*

MIRANDA. Here it is! Here it is!

WILMA. What's it say?

MIRANDA. "L.S. is not Lenora Stark." I need to find Holly right away. Lock the door after I leave.

(*She produces the gun that the deputy gave her.*)

THURMIN. Will that gun really be necessary?

MIRANDA. I hope not.

(**MIRANDA** *exits through the bedroom door.* **WILMA** *locks it.*)

WILMA. She'll be alright.

THURMIN. I'm not sure any of us will be.

WILMA. What else could "L.S." mean?

THURMIN. I have no idea.

(**HOLLY** *backs into the living room, alone. She has heard a noise.* **MIRANDA** *enters and frightens her.*)

HOLLY. Oh, it's you.

MIRANDA. I'm sorry I didn't mean to frighten you. Where is the deputy?

HOLLY. She told me to come down here. She went to check out a noise in the attic.

MIRANDA. Someone in this house is trying to tell us something. Read this.

HOLLY. "L.S." is not Lenora Stark." Doesn't stand for Lenora Stark? A woman is stabbed in the throat with scissors. Her last act alive is to write the letters "L.S." on the wall in her own blood. Letters that just happen to be the initials of her only daughter. And you are telling me that these letters do not stand for "Lenora Stark"?

MIRANDA. It's not me that's telling you that.

HOLLY. This was the most damning piece of evidence. What else could it mean? We could check the church records and see if there is anyone with those initials.

(*They look about the room.*)

MIRANDA. Maybe it stands for something in this room. Light stand. Lamp shade. Maybe one of the paintings. Or the initials of one of the artists.

(They begin to study the paintings.)

HOLLY. Problem is, none of the paintings are titled or signed. I'm not very fluent in religious art.

MIRANDA. *(in front of a painting)* Everyone knows the title of this painting. "The Last Supper."

HOLLY. "The Last Supper." It can't be that simple. Why didn't anyone think of that?

MIRANDA. It just made so much sense that the victim would write the name of her attacker on the wall in her own blood.

(They quickly pull the painting off the wall.)

HOLLY. Nothing behind it.

MIRANDA. Give me that.

(She pulls the print out of the frame. An envelope falls to the floor. She picks it up and opens it.)

Money. A lot of money. And a note.

*(She hands the note to **HOLLY**.)*

HOLLY. "Dear Lenora, Take this money and get Abigale out of here. Go to the train station and buy two tickets. Go far away and change your name. He's never going to stop and he may do worse. We're going to be at the church tomorrow all day. Always know that I love you. And I am sorry. Love, Mom."

(pause)

She was killed before she could ever tell Lenora what she hid behind this painting. What's more, there was an Abigale and this letter proves it.

MIRANDA. There is an Abigale, you mean. Then that's why Lenora broke out of the asylum.

HOLLY. She's come home to stop her sister.

MIRANDA. Yes. But, if Abigale killed Gretchen…

> *(There is a loud bang.)*

…which one of us is Abigale?

DEPUTY TERRY. *(enters)* We didn't find anything. What have you got there?

HOLLY. *(handing her the letter)* You better read this.

> *(**DEPUTY TERRY** reads the letter.)*

DEPUTY TERRY. This changes everything.

> *(blackout)*

Scene Two

(SETTING: The same.)

(AT RISE: Five minutes later. The women are standing around the card table, reading Mrs. Stark's letter to **LENORA**.*)*

THURMIN. It's a fake. Do you know how easy it would be to fake a 13 year-old letter? I mean, how convenient. I'll grant you the 'L.S' "Last Supper" business is clever. But, come on. We're not idiots here. Hey, I bet that's why Anthony broke in here, to plant this letter.

HOLLY. Then who killed him and why?

THURMIN. I didn't say I had all the answers.

MIRANDA. We're not going to know if this letter is genuine until it's looked at by a handwriting expert. Even if it is the real deal and Abigale did exist, that's not proof she killed the Starks.

INGRID. Yes, but at the very least, proving Abigale's existence raises reasonable doubt. They'd have to over-turn Lenora's conviction.

WILMA. Yeah, but she still killed a prison guard.

INGRID. We don't know that for sure. Another woman escaped with her.

WILMA. Yeah, and she ended-up dead, too.

HOLLY. I don't know what to think anymore.

(DEPUTY TERRY enters carrying the walkie-talkie.)

DEPUTY TERRY. Sheriff Watkins is doing his best to get help out here. He's contacted the State Troopers and the FBI. I've up-dated him on all developments and he wants us to sit tight until help gets here. Oh, and he said I can return your belongings.

(She empties an old duffel bag on the sofa.)

HOLLY. What's all this?

DEPUTY TERRY. It's the stuff Gretchen stole from you.

WILMA. Gretchen ripped us off?

DEPUTY TERRY. It appears that way.

WILMA. I can't believe she would do that to us. We pick her up from the side of the road and give her safe place to stay.

THURMIN. Not that safe as it turns out.

WILMA. Well, still she didn't have to steal from us.

DEPUTY TERRY. It's possible Gretchen was trying to get out of here when she was killed. Go ahead and claim your belongings.

THURMIN. Isn't this evidence? Aren't you supposed to take this to the station?

DEPUTY TERRY. For what? The trial?

THURMIN. That woman robbed us! There are procedures!

DEPUTY TERRY. I'm pretty sure she won't do it again.

HOLLY. Hey, people. Focus. Gretchen is dead. We've got bigger problems here.

MIRANDA. Holly is right. Deputy Terry, isn't it possible that one of us here is Abigale?

DEPUTY TERRY. I've thought of that.

MIRANDA. How old would Abigale be?

DEPUTY TERRY. Around 25, give or take a few years.

MIRANDA. That leaves me out.

WILMA. Me, Ingrid, and the deputy aren't twenty-five and well, obviously Mrs. Thurmin isn't twenty-five.

DEPUTY TERRY. Since they didn't observe birthdays and Lenora's testimony was sketchy about when Abigale was born, it's hard to say.

THURMIN. So, someone in this room could be the killer?

DEPUTY TERRY. Anything's possible.

THURMIN. Holly, how old are you?

HOLLY. Twenty-five.

THURMIN. That's the magic number, isn't it? You also mentioned that you had several foster parents. What happened to your real parents, Holly?

HOLLY. Car crash.

THURMIN. And this book you supposedly became acquainted with the Stark family murders from, according to your own friends, doesn't even exist.

WILMA. I just said I couldn't find it, that's all. That doesn't mean the book doesn't exist.

THURMIN. Leaves one to wonder how she became such an expert on the murders. Almost a first-hand account, if you ask me.

MIRANDA. How old was Gretchen?

INGRID. I don't know, she could have been 25. She knew Abigale's real age, remember?

DEPUTY TERRY. Maybe she was just good at math.

WILMA. Or maybe she knows how old she was. Lenora gets in the house finds Abigale, and kills her. Maybe that's all she came to do. End of story.

(They all start arguing at once.)

THURMIN. Stop it! Stop it! This is getting us nowhere! There is a dead body in the house and one of you killed her! I want you all to stay away from me! Stay away!

(She flees from the room.)

HOLLY. Mrs. Thurmin, no! Deputy Terry, we should go after her. You said we should stick together.

DEPUTY TERRY. Right. Let's all go. Just make sure you stick with someone and don't get left behind.

*(They all run off in different directions. **LENORA** quietly enters and picks up the letter. She reads it. And cries. She crosses to the blood stains on the wall and traces the initials gently with her finger. Taking the letter with her, she sneaks off. We hear shouts of "Mrs. Thurmin" throughout the house. **MIRANDA** and **WILMA** enter.)*

WILMA. She's nowhere. How could she disappear so fast?

MIRANDA. I don't know. She can't get very far in this storm.

INGRID. *(entering)* Did you find her?

MIRANDA. No sign of her. You?

INGRID. No. We looked everywhere.

WILMA. I don't like this.

INGRID. Where's Holly?

WILMA. I thought she was with you!

INGRID. I thought she was with you!

HOLLY. *(dazed, enters)* Here I am.

INGRID. What happened to you?

HOLLY. In a dark hallway, someone ran past me and knocked me down.

MIRANDA. Who was it?

HOLLY. It was dark. I couldn't tell. They were being chased, or chasing someone. I hit my head I think…

INGRID. *(crossing to her)* Are you alright?

HOLLY. I think so.

MIRANDA. Holly, your hands. They're covered in blood.

HOLLY. Oh, yes. I must have cut myself when I fell down

INGRID. Here's some paper towels. Let's try and stop the bleeding.

HOLLY. *(wiping her hands)* Thank you.

(**MIRANDA**, **WILMA** *and* **INGRID** *all exchange glances.*)

MIRANDA. Holly, did you see Deputy Terry?

HOLLY. No. I don't think so.

INGRID. Holly, this isn't your blood.

HOLLY. It's not?

INGRID. No. Your hands aren't injured. Holly, Who' s blood is on you?

HOLLY. I don't know. Someone bumped into me in a dark hall. I already told you that.

WILMA. I wonder where the deputy is.

DEPUTY TERRY. *(Enters, carrying a pail, which she places on the card table.)* I'm right here.

(She sits down at the desk. She is visibly shaken.)

We are in very deep trouble.

INGRID. Did you find Mrs. Thurmin?

DEPUTY TERRY. Part of her.

WILMA. Part of her? What does that mean?

DEPUTY TERRY. I only found part of her.

HOLLY. What are you saying?

DEPUTY TERRY. She's dead.

INGRID. How can you be so sure?

> (**DEPUTY TERRY** *indicates the bucket.*)

What could possibly be in that bucket that would make you think that Mrs. Thurmin is dead?

DEPUTY TERRY. You're welcome to take a look. I wouldn't advise it. But I think it's important for our survival that you trust me.

INGRID. This is absurd. I mean, even if it is a body part, how are you so sure that it's Mrs. Thurmin?

> (*The* **DEPUTY** *indicates the bucket again. The lights go out.*)

WILMA. I told you the generator was making funny noises.

> (*One by one the ladies turn on their flashlights. The women slowly approach the silver pail. Shining their lights into the pail, the women scream.*)
>
> (*blackout*)

Scene Three

(*SETTING: The same.*)

(*AT RISE: Three minutes later.* **INGRID** *is on the couch and the others are gathered around her. She suddenly sits up with a scream.*)

INGRID. Is it still in here?

DEPUTY TERRY. No, no. We got rid of it.

INGRID. Where is it?

DEPUTY TERRY. It doesn't matter. You never have to see it again.

INGRID. Where did you find it?

DEPUTY TERRY. The killer placed it on the kitchen table.

INGRID. Who could do that to another human being? It's all so insane.

HOLLY. We're not going to survive in the dark.

DEPUTY TERRY. Wilma, do you think you can fix the generator?

WILMA. I can try.

DEPUTY TERRY. Alright, Miranda and I will go with you to watch your back and help if we can. Okay?

MIRANDA. Fine by me.

DEPUTY TERRY. Let's go. The killers only chance is to separate us. You two stick together.

HOLLY. We will.

(**DEPUTY TERRY,** **MIRANDA** *and* **WILMA** *exit out the stage left door.*)

You see what she's doing, don't you?

INGRID. What who is doing?

HOLLY. The killer. Gretchen was stabbed in the throat by scissors just like Mrs. Stark. Rev. Stark was decapitated…

INGRID. Just like Mrs. Thurmin. You think she's repeating the murders. Someone is repeating the murders, but it isn't Lenora. It's Abigale. I met Lenora. She's here. I spoke with her. She told me everything.

HOLLY. What? When? How?

INGRID. In my room when you were searching the house with Deputy Terry. She's here to stop Abigale.

HOLLY. No, Ingrid. Lenora is not here. It was just a dream. You must have fallen asleep.

INGRID. No, she's real. I saw her!

(Suddenly the walkie-talkie begins to squawk.)

INGRID. Deputy Terry left the walkie-talkie.

HOLLY. *(picking it up)* Sheriff Watkins! Sheriff Watkins! Are you there? We need help!

(There is a lot of static but a few words get through.)

INGRID. I can't understand him.

HOLLY. Say again, Sheriff!

SHERIFF WATKINS. I need to speak to Deputy Terry.

HOLLY. *(yelling)* She went outside to fix the generator! I repeat she went outside to fix the generator! We'll go get her!

SHERIFF WATKINS. *(static but a few urgent words get thru)* The deputy needs…before….

HOLLY. Say again, Sheriff! It must be the storm. You keep breaking up! I can't hear you!

SHERIFF WATKINS. Is Deputy Terry there? I need to speak to him.

(static)

I need to speak to him!!

(The women stare at one another. The static gets unbearably loud.)

HOLLY. If you can hear me, Sheriff Watkins, get here as fast as you can!

*(The walkie-talkie goes dead. **HOLLY** tries desperately to activate it. The lights come on. The others return.)*

DEPUTY TERRY. What are you doing with that?

HOLLY. The Sheriff was looking for you.

DEPUTY TERRY. Did you talk to him?

HOLLY. No. We couldn't hear each other.

>*(pause)*

WILMA. At least we have lights again.

MIRANDA. *(handing the deputy her gun)* Here. Take this thing. I'm too jumpy. I almost shot the generator when it started up. I'm gonna kill somebody with this.

HOLLY. No!!!

INGRID. *(at the same time)* No!

DEPUTY TERRY. *(taking the gun)* What's going on here?

HOLLY. Nothing. It just makes sense for two people to be armed, is all.

INGRID. Yeah. Twice as much protection.

HOLLY. I'll take the gun. I've used a gun before.

>(**DEPUTY TERRY** *begins to hand the gun to* **HOLLY** *then takes it back.)*

DEPUTY TERRY. Come to think of it, I am going to need both guns now.

>*(aiming her gun at them)*

>Everybody sit down.

>*(They do.)*

WILMA. What's going on?

HOLLY. Abigale wants us to sit down.

WILMA. Abigale?

ABIGALE (DEPUTY TERRY). *(smiling)* How did you figure it out?

HOLLY. I just lied to you. I did speak to Sheriff Watkins on the walkie-talkie and he told me why you can't be Deputy Terry. He's on his way out here.

ABIGALE. That still gives me plenty of time for my ending.

INGRID. I don't get it. How were you able to impersonate the deputy? I don't understand how the Sheriff wouldn't recognize his own deputy.

ABIGALE. *(She slowly slips into a childlike state from this point to end of play.)* Sheriff Watkins did send a deputy out here. You'll find him hanging from a tree behind the privy. Once I saw the name on his name tag was Terry and his clothes fit, I figured that since you were interested in making a play, I could be an actress, too. Wasn't that smart of me?

MIRANDA. Very clever, Abigale.

ABIGALE. Of course I never actually talked to the Sheriff on the walkie-talkie. I was just pretending.

MIRANDA. You fooled us all.

ABIGALE. Yes, I did fool you. I fooled all of you.

INGRID. Wait. You were in this room with us when Gretchen screamed.

ABIGALE. Yes. If you remember, I was the most surprised of all, because I had just stabbed Gretchen in the throat with a pair of scissors. So I told you all to stay here and went back to the kitchen to finish the job. Next time I'll use a bigger pair of scissors.

INGRID. Why kill Gretchen at all? And Mrs. Thurmin?

ABIGALE. I have to kill all of you. As long as I keep people out of this house no one can hurt me.

WILMA. I can understand killing the Starks after what happened to you. I really can. But why all this?

ABIGALE. You came here to blame me for what happened. Just like Anthony did. You came here to find proof to get Lenny out of jail. I can't let that happen. She deserves to rot in jail for what she did. She let those things happen to me. She was old enough to save me and she didn't. She made me think that she cared about me.

HOLLY. It was very ingenious of a 12 year-old girl to frame Lenora that way.

ABIGALE. Ingenious? I didn't plan it. She just wasn't home. If she were, I would have killed her too. I decided to break out of the barn and run away. I overheard Rev. Stark talking about doing something with me. I didn't want to wait around and see what that was. I started digging a tunnel in one of the old un-used horse stalls at the back of the barn, during the night. Nobody ever went back there.

(pause)

The earth was pretty soft, so the digging was pretty easy. Until I found the first bone. Then another. And another, and bloody sheets. Old bloody sheets the color of rust. And finally a human skull. The skull was wrapped in an old faded ripped blanket. I recognized the blanket as being the other half of the torn blanket I always had with me.

(pause)

Even at 12 years old, I realized that I had un-earthed all that was left of my mother. It finally made sense to me.

(pause)

At first I was just trying to escape and then after I found my mother, all that mattered was punishing those that did that to her. I found the axe in the back hall and well…the Starks learned how mad I could get. He was at his desk. I told him, "This is for my mother." I started hitting him with the axe. I kept hitting until the blade of the axe got stuck in his back and snapped off the handle.

(pause)

Mrs. Stark was in the basement doing laundry. I heard her coming up the stairs. She came into the room carrying a laundry basket and actually slipped on the blood and fell down. The clothes and basket went flying. She made this little "Ooooh" sound. It was funny. I started to laugh. She didn't think it was funny, though. She started to scream when she saw what I did. She tried to crawl into the next room. I grabbed the scissors from her sewing basket. She didn't make it.

HOLLY. Where did you go? How were you able to survive? You were just a child.

ABIGALE. I hopped the train and ended-up in New York City. I met this man on a dark street corner. A man of business. The Reverend had taught me well. I made the business man a lot of money. Sometimes I had to punish the clients. Sometimes they hurt me and they had to be punished. When I was 16, I punished the businessman.

MIRANDA. I'm so sorry, Abigale. You never had a chance.

ABIGALE. That's right. I never had a chance.

HOLLY. The grounds were searched for your mother's remains, how come they were never found?

ABIGALE. I took mother with me. I couldn't leave her here. Not my mother.

WILMA. What are you going to do after you kill all of us?

ABIGALE. I'm going to go look for Lenny and kill her too.

INGRID. Lenora's here.

ABIGALE. You're just trying to trick me.

INGRID. She is. I spoke to her. Lenny told me she came here to help you. She loves you. She told me how she snuck you into her room on cold nights and how she told you a bed time story every night.

ABIGALE. Shut up!

MIRANDA. Abigale, she's telling the truth. I had a dream last night, a vision really, it was just like this. I was sitting here, you were standing there with your gun and Lenora walks through that door.

ABIGALE. A vision, huh? What are you psychic or something?

MIRANDA. Yes, Abigale. I see things, just like you do. And I saw Lenora coming for you.

ABIGALE. Did you see this coming?

(*She shoots* **MIRANDA.** **MIRANDA** *places her hands on her stomach and holds up bloody hands.* **LENORA** *enters.*)

LENORA. Abbey! What have you done?

ABIGALE. Lenny? Lenny, is that really you?

LENORA. Abbey, put that gun down at once! Don't be a bad girl!

ABIGALE. I won't put it down! You want to hurt me! You all want to hurt me!

LENORA. I am not going to hurt you, Abbey. I love you, Abbey.

ABIGALE. You knew what he was doing to me. At night. Out in the barn. In the dark. You knew what he was doing.

LENORA. I didn't know, Abbey. I didn't know for sure. But he's gone now, and he can't hurt you anymore.

(**HOLLY** *and* **INGRID** *rush to* **MIRANDA**'s *aid. Using a wad of paper towels they manage to stop the bleeding.*)

ABIGALE. You killed my mother. My real mother.

LENORA. It wasn't me, Abbey. I would never do such a thing. You must believe me. You know who killed your mother and you already punished him.

ABIGALE. You all want to hurt me. I can't let you. It stops right here and right now.

LENORA. Abbey, no!

(**LENORA** *lunges at* **ABIGALE** *and grabs the gun. The two struggle. The gun goes off.* **ABIGALE** *slowly drops to the sofa.*)

(*to* **HOLLY**) Get your friend to the hospital! It's not too late.

HOLLY. The tires on the van are slashed.

LENORA. Use the police car. The keys are in it.

INGRID. It's in a ditch.

LENORA. She lied! It's parked down the road. The bridge is safe, too. Go, quickly before it's too late. Hurry!

(*The others carry* **MIRANDA** *off.* **LENORA** *locks the door and barricades it with a chair.* **LENORA** *sits beside her sister on the sofa and wraps her arms around her.*)

ABIGALE. I'm bleeding. I'm bleeding.

LENORA. Yes.

(*pause*)

It feels so good to have you in my arms again.

ABIGALE. Yes. It's the only place I ever felt safe.

LENORA. Abbey. Abbey, I'm so sorry.

ABIGALE. Lenny, why didn't you save me?

LENORA. I couldn't even save myself, baby. I am so sorry. So very sorry.

ABIGALE. I guess we know the ending of our fairy tale now, don't we?

LENORA. No, Abbey. This is not the end. It can't be. It can't work that way.

ABIGALE. Then, what comes next?

LENORA. Somehow, someway, my baby, we'll get another chance.

ABIGALE. (*She smiles.*) I'd like another chance. Will it hurt, Lenny?

LENORA. It won't be the kind of hurt we are used to.

ABIGALE. I'm cold.

LENORA. I know, baby.

(**LENORA** *rises and gets a stick of fire from the fireplace and places it under the sofa. She sits beside her sister again. Smoke begins to seep up from the sofa cushions.*)

It won't be long now.

ABIGALE. You won't let go of me this time, will you Lenny?

LENORA. No, Abbey. I will never let go of you again. I promise.

ABIGALE. And they both lived happily ever-after…

LENORA. And they both lived happily ever-after.

(*She cradles her sister in her arms and hums a tender lullaby as the sofa catches fire.*)

(*blackout*)

End of Play

THE SET

Three raised platforms serve as two bedrooms and a small section of attic. In the original production we used 8 foot high platforms to give the illusion of a two story house, but shorter platforms, upstage of the main acting space, would serve as well. Because the house is abandoned, there is no furniture in the bedrooms. The women sit on their sleeping bags on the floor. Both bedrooms have a door that can close. No staircases are visible. The attic space was small and shadowy and contained only a rocking chair, a trunk and two dress dummies wearing old fashioned wedding gowns.

Set decoration: We created the look of old faded wallpaper in all the rooms, but the most dramatic effect was the over 100 pictures of religious art on the set. Not only does this create an extremely unsettling look, but it helps hide the reprint of "The Last Supper" which we made a smaller painting mixed in with the several on the wall.

COSTUMES

MIRANDA - a colorful, floor length and flowing skirt; a loose fitting blouse, a dramatic neck scarf and head scarf, a faded denim jacket.

WILMA - blue jeans, thermal t-shirt, flannel shirt, work boots.

INGRID - blue jeans, sweatshirt, sneakers.

HOLLY - dark slacks, turtle neck, button-up sweater with pockets, dark shoes

MRS. THURMIN - a conservative polyester pantsuit, high-collar blouse and sensible shoes

GRETCHEN - ripped and faded jeans, denim work shirt, black leather jacket, black motorcycle boots.

DEPUTY TERRY - tan uniform pants and long sleeve shirt. Uniform brown jacket with silver badge. Holster and gun.

LENORA STARK - bright orange prison jumpsuit covered in blood. Black shoes.

PROPS

Book
diary
sewing basket
plastic axe
metal tray
paper cups
scissors
Polaroid camera
envelope of crime scene photos
walkie-talkie
transistor radio
tape measure
6 flashlights
6 sleeping bags
2 suitcases
3 backpacks
1 old duffle bag
candle
jack-o lantern with flickering bulb
sewing basket with fabric to cut
large pair of silver scissors
deck of Tarot cards
3 coffee mugs
2 prop revolvers
bloody towel
sketch pad and pencils
an envelope containing a faded letter
silver pail
roll of paper towels
stick from the fireplace.

SPECIAL EFFECTS

The fire in the fireplace; we inserted a flat screen television set into our fireplace opening and played a recorded DVD fire.

The burning couch: We installed 2 fog machines under the couch and used flickering lights from over head to create the illusion of flames. Because the couch is old and ratty we created many holes in the fabric where the fog could rise up.

We recorded Sheriff Watkins and the Radio Broadcaster dialogue. We installed a small speaker in the card table and made sure the walkie talkie always stayed near the card table to make it seem like the Sheriff's voice was coming from the walkie talkie. Likewise, the transistor radio sat on the fireplace where we hid another small speaker. These roles could be performed live offstage through a microphone.

Mrs. Thurmin uses a large pair of shiny silver scissors that reflect the stage lights. It is very erie when she sits there cutting out fabric and the audience hears that sinister snick-snick. Later when the scissors are presented in a bloody white towel as the murder weapon it creates a wonderfully chilling moment. It is recommended that you use silver spray paint on a plastic pair of scissors to avoid injury!

The silver pail, of course, is empty! Nothing you could place in it would equal the audiences' vivid imagination!

OTHER TITLES AVAILABLE FROM BAKER'S PLAYS

DEATH BY ARRANGEMENT

David Alberts

Mystery / 7m, 4f / Interior

Nothing is as it seems in this intriguing, amusing, and devilishly deceptive murder mystery! Set in present-day London, the plot revolves around the death of one Mr. Evan MacKenzie, and a houseful of suspects — everyone from his lovely widow to the lowly kitchen maid, each with his or her own motive and opportunity. Pity Detective Sergeant Benson, who must assemble the elusive pieces of the puzzle in this stylish whodunit. Everyone comes under his careful scrutiny, but he is misled and outwitted again and again until finally, as he leads his prime suspect off to jail, we learn the identity of the real murderer! A mistaken identity, a "fatal substance," and unexpected twists and turns will keep your audience guessing and hanging onto the edges of their seats until the final curtain. A play with subtlety, great humor and well-defined characters in the classic tradition of great stage mysteries.

OTHER TITLES AVAILABLE FROM BAKER'S PLAYS

IF SHERLOCK HOLMES WERE A WOMAN

Tim Kelly

Mystery Comedy / 7f / Interior

Shirley Holmes is named after the famous sleuth of Sir Arthur Conan Doyle fame. She is a fanatic on mystery and crime. Her big chance comes when the housemother in her dorm is found dead under peculiar circumstances. Shirley, determined to solve the crime, locks all the girls in the communal study. The suspects include Melanie, the professional southern Belle; Sniffles the hypochondriac; Theda, the world's greatest undiscovered talent; and Fifi, an exchange student whose biggest battle is understanding English. Shirley has a noble assistant in "Dotty" Watson, who is delighted to write everything down in her "memoirs." Shirley's sleuthing is hilarious and causes something of a scandal as she unravels the "heinous crime."